THE ZEPHYR CONSPIRACY

THE ZEPHYR CONSPIRACY

ISRAEL KEATS

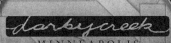

darbycreek

MINNEAPOLIS

Darby Creek
A division of Lerner Publishing Group, Inc.
241 First Avenue North
Minneapolis, MN 55401 USA

For reading levels and more information, look up this title at www.lernerbooks.com.

Images in this book used with the permission of: © Atelier Sommerland/Shutterstock.com (zephyr), © iStockphoto.com/Thoth_Adan (grunge background).

Main body text set in Janson Text LT Std 12/17.5.
Typeface provided by Adobe Systems.

Library of Congress Cataloging-in-Publication Data

The Cataloging-in-Publication Data for The Zephyr Conspiracy is on file at the Library of Congress.
ISBN 978-1-5124-3985-4 (lib. bdg.)
ISBN 978-1-5124-5361-4 (pbk.)
ISBN 978-1-5124-4874-0 (EB pdf)

Manufactured in the United States of America
1-42234-25783-3/7/2017

To Jules Verne

It is the year 2089. Virtual reality games are part of everyday life, and one company—L33T CORP—is behind the most popular games. Though most people are familiar with L33T CORP, few know much about what happens behind the scenes of the megacorporation.

L33T CORP has developed a new virtual reality game: *Level Up*. It contains more than one thousand unique virtual realities for gamers to play. But the company needs testers to smooth out glitches. Teenagers from around the country are chosen for this task and, suddenly, they find themselves in the middle of a video game. The company gives them a warning—win the game, or be trapped within it. Forever.

CHAPTER 1

The gamer appeared on a sky deck in a city of
skyscrapers, the L33T C0RP logo glowing under
her feet. Most of the buildings in this city were
as tall as this one, and they had the decorative
style of old buildings. There were carvings on
the panels and designs worked into the columns.
It looked both high tech and old-fashioned, like a
city of the future if it existed in 1890.

    Steampunk, she thought. *I like it already.*

    She carefully moved to the edge of the
deck and peered over. It was about a thousand
feet to the ground. She could barely see the
streets through the web of rails and walkways
connecting the buildings.

I wonder what kind of vehicle travels on those rails.

In the distance she saw one building towering over the rest. Its tinted glass walls shone like jewels. At the peak of its highest tower was a tremendous clock that showed the time as two minutes before noon—or midnight—but neither was true. The sun was just rising across the skyline.

"How do you like the game so far?" a voice behind her asked. She turned to see a man wearing a white suit and sunglasses.

"It's incredible. Like the past and the future merged together," she said.

"That's the point," he agreed. "I'm the Game Runner. What do you want to call yourself?"

"I usually use Gadget," she replied.

"Is that because you like gadgets?"

"Yep. I like to tinker—take things apart and see how they work."

"Then I think you're going to like this game," he said. "Unless you're afraid of heights?"

"Nope," she said. "Just afraid of falling."

He nodded and chuckled at her joke, then waved his hand at her shirt. She looked down and saw her gamertag appear in scarlet stitches on a black vest that had shiny buttons. She hadn't noticed her outfit until just now. She was also wearing red leggings, black boots, and a white tunic. A leather bag was slung across her shoulder, but when she patted it she could tell it was empty. A belt around her waist held a scabbard with a small curved sword.

"I'm dressed like a sailor," Gadget said, looking up. "I should be at sea, not in a city."

"You *are* a sailor," he said, "but your sea is the sky." He waved a hand with a flourish. The bow of a ship peeked through the clouds, and then the whole ship burst through the white fluff. It looked like a ship from two hundred years ago, but in place of sails it had an enormous football-shaped balloon.

"That is the airship *Zephyr*," the Game Runner explained. "It's captained by the infamous pirate, Weston Fawkes Junior. It also happens to be where you live and work."

"So I'm a pirate in this game?"

"A pirate in training," he corrected. "You're currently a deckhand. Your goal is to make your way up through the ranks. Well, that's one goal. There are many ways to play this game. Do you want to become the captain of the *Zephyr*? Betray your crew to the Verne Aero-Navy? Sneak off with the loot? Those are all possibilities. It's up to you."

"What's Verne?" Gadget asked.

"The city before you," he explained. "It's a rich world with hundreds of adventures and thousands of characters."

"It's so big. I'll never explore it all in one game."

"This game is meant to be re-played, again and again, and never be the same," he said. "Not only can you play one story in many different ways, but you can also start out as several different characters with different goals. But *you* only get one story now, and you know what happens if you lose."

She nodded. "I stay here forever. At least I wouldn't get bored, right?"

"Unless you end up in prison," he said. "Or get captured by a rival pirate crew. There are lots of possibilities. Including death. If you die in this game, you're done. There's no respawning."

She gulped. "Gotcha." *The game is re-playable, but only if I win the first time.*

"Also, this is a multiplayer game," the Game Runner continued. "You'll encounter both human players and non-player characters, or NPCs, that you may choose to work with."

Ugh. I hate working in groups, she thought, *in games or in school. I end up doing all the work while the others take the credit.* Her face must have shown her feelings.

"You don't seem excited about this."

"I guess I find machines easier to figure out than people."

"You'll be fine. With the NPCs, at least. Just figure out what they want and give it to them."

"How do I know if someone is real or an NPC?"

"That's for you to figure out," he said. "But you know, real people aren't much different to deal with."

A long rope ladder dropped down from the airship. A scruffy young man appeared above the rear of the ship and waved a sword.

"It's time for you to get started," the Game Runner said as he slowly faded away.

LEVEL 1

CHAPTER 2

"Climb aboard, milady!" shouted the teenaged boy at the railing.

Milady? Pretty fancy way to say it's time to scrub the deck, she thought. Then she reminded herself that this was a steampunk game, a world filled with "gentlemen pirates." She grabbed the rope ladder and started to climb. The ladder swayed and buckled in the wind. *My joke about falling already isn't funny anymore.*

Gadget kept climbing, feeling her body swing back and forth. She finally reached the top, and the boy helped her over the rail. He looked slightly older than she was, with a few wispy whiskers on his unshaven face. He was wearing a sailing outfit that was similar to hers, though he also wore a sophisticated navy blue coat that had big brass buttons. She saw his name embroidered on his coat: *TerribleT.* But he didn't look that terrible.

I'll call you Terry, she thought.

"Come on," he said. "There's a meeting on the main deck."

She followed Terry across the rear deck. At the end it dropped off to a lower deck. About twenty pirates were gathered there. For pirates, they were surprisingly well dressed in long coats with high collars and lots of shiny buttons. Some wore high-waisted pants and vests, and on top of their heads others wore goggles or top hats.

Can I trust any of them? she wondered. *Can I even get along with them? I've never been great at compromising.*

A short man climbed up on a barrel. "Hello, gentlemen and ladies!" he cried in a high voice, sounding overly formal.

"Hello, Captain Fawkes!" The pirates waved their top hats and hands in the air as they cheered.

Doesn't seem very scary, as far as pirate captains go, she thought. He was too short and too polite.

"Are there any treasure hunters among us?" asked the captain as the noise died down.

The group whooped again, louder than before.

"I'll take that as a yes, so listen up." The captain unrolled a map and held it up for all to see. It was a sprawling city with an ocean on one side and mountains on the other. Gadget tried to get a better look, but there were too many people jostling in front of her.

"This map belonged to my father," he said. "As you know, the Aero-Navy caught him several years ago . . ."

The pirates booed. *His dad must be Weston Fawkes Senior,* thought Gadget.

"The Aero-Navy *stole* this map from him," the pirate captain told the crew. "Fortunately, I have a friend on the inside, and he stole it back. Take a look. Right here's the city of Verne. You can see there are *X* marks all over it. My father told me that he scattered different treasures around the city in eight safes."

The pirates fell to a hush.

"Here's where you come in. We want to explore all these spots before the Aero-Navy finds out the map is missing. Some have treasure and some don't. All we know is that they were points of interest for my dearly departed father."

The group of pirates were nodding and whispering to one another.

"You may work in teams," the captain added. "Half of anything you find is mine and the other half is yours to divvy up. If you want to plunder another team's loot or betray your own comrades, well, that's what pirates do." The pirates cheered and laughed.

He waved at the group to quiet down. "One last thing: anyone who doesn't find treasure will be a minion for life!" The captain hopped off the barrel, signaling he was finished. The pirates quickly huddled up in small groups to plot and scheme.

Gadget now found a roll of paper in her bag. *The magic of the game*, she thought. *We all get a copy of the map.* She unrolled it and studied it. There were dozens of X marks strewn across the city. *Some have treasure but most are probably dead ends,* she figured. *Which do I try first?*

Somebody nudged her elbow. She turned and saw Terry. "Looking for a partner?" he asked.

"Um—" *He seems all right, and I don't know if I can do this alone.* "Sure. But it has to be just us. Nobody else."

He frowned. "Two is a small group if it comes to fighting. Maybe we should join a team."

"We're a couple of deckhands. I'm hoping they'll forget we even exist."

"Hm. Maybe you're right," he said, nodding.

Together they looked at the map in Gadget's hands. "Let's go here," she said, pointing at the X mark that was the farthest away.

"It looks like it's up in the mountains," Terry said.

"Exactly. The others will try for the easier spots first, so we can try the harder ones without running into rival teams."

"That makes sense," he said. "But how do we get there?"

"I don't know."

He snapped his fingers. "I saw a broken cloud-skimmer down in the hold. If we fix it we can sail over to that cliff."

"Let's do it." *I don't know what a cloud-skimmer is, but I'm sure I'll figure it out when I see it. I don't want him thinking I'm a n00b and don't know what I'm doing.*

While the other pirates were still getting into groups, Terry led Gadget through a trap door in the main deck. They crept down a ladder without anyone noticing and crawled through the darkness between barrels and crates. Only a few narrow slashes of light shone through the cracks in the boards over their heads.

I bet Terry is a real player, she thought. *I wonder how long he's been here.*

Terry stopped in a corner and pointed to a contraption that looked like a bronze and leather wheelless motorcycle with folded wings on each side. Gadget pulled it out and found a button. When she pushed the button, the wings unfolded. They looked like bat wings made of black fabric stretched across a metal skeleton. On the rear side was something that looked like a propeller, which was fastened with wing nuts she could remove by hand.

"I can take this off to get at the motor," she said. "But I won't be able to see a thing."

"Let me find a light." Terry disappeared and returned with a lantern.

Behind the propeller was a panel. She opened it and saw a complex series of gears and a rubber belt that had come undone. Fortunately the belt wasn't broken, but it wasn't clear how it fit around the posts that turned the gears.

Of course not. It's a puzzle, she realized. But there were little arrows on the posts showing which way they should turn, and she knew she'd have to feed the belt over or under the posts so the gears would move in the right direction. She tried it a couple of different ways before the belt seemed tight enough to work but not so tight it would snap.

At last she slammed the panel shut. "Let's give it a try," she said. They hauled the machine out of the hold. It would have been heavy for one person to carry but was easy with two.

The deck was now empty.

"Everybody else took off," Terry said.

"How did they leave?"

"They used the sky-skiffs," he said, pointing at an empty rack. "Smaller airships, powered by mini gasbags." *That must be what the airship's balloon is called—a gasbag*, thought Gadget. "There are four sky-skiffs, so there must be four teams."

"Got it," she said. She unfolded the wings on their machine. "What's this called again?"

"A cloud-skimmer," he said. She turned it on and it came to life with a purr.

Terry cheered with a loud whoop. "You fixed it!"

"Get on," she said. "We have treasure to find."

CHAPTER 3

The cloud-skimmer was meant for one person, but they were still able to fit on the seat together, as if they were riding a motorcycle. Gadget sat in front, pulling on the two handlebars to steer, and Terry was behind her. They cruised across the sky, weaving between spires and towers, veering left and right to avoid colliding with bigger aircraft. As they hit the outskirts of Verne, the air was more open.

The *X* on the map was between two mountain peaks. Gadget saw the peaks now and headed for them. As she got closer she saw a large, run-down Victorian-style mansion. But it was big even for a mansion—about twenty stories high.

"It must be there!" she shouted and leaned forward to descend. It occurred to her that she had no idea how to brake. The cloud-skimmer gained speed as she approached. They were about to crash into the building.

"Stop!" Terry screamed behind her.

"I don't know how!" She looked desperately for controls.

"Use your feet!"

For most of their trip, she had let her feet dangle off the sides of the vehicle. She now saw footrests and stretched her legs, finding the pedals and pushing them moments before the cloud-skimmer smashed into the front of the building. A parachute puffed out behind them and they slowed, striking the side of the building but bouncing back unharmed. The machine spun as they dropped and hit the ground with a bump.

"Maybe I'll drive from now on," Terry said.

Gadget rolled her eyes. "Now that I know where the brakes are, I'll be fine."

They got off the cloud-skimmer and looked up at the big mansion. It must have been white at some time but was now muddy and gray. Shingles had been blown off the steep roof, probably long ago. There were cobwebs in the windows. A tower rose high on one side and leaned to the left. It looked like it would collapse the next time there was a hard wind.

A sign was staked in the lawn. The paint had faded but she could still read it:

WELCOME TO THE BENBOW INN

"Better find out what's in there before it falls down," she said.

"Try not to breathe on it," Terry joked, but he followed her to the entrance.

The boards creaked as they walked up the sagging porch and pushed open the front door.

"Baggage?" a wooden bellhop asked when they entered. It looked like a life-sized wooden toy that walked and talked. It was at least seven feet tall and wide enough to block the door. Its red hat looked tiny on its enormous head.

"Where's your baggage?" the bellhop asked again.

"We don't have any," Gadget said.

"You must have baggage," the bellhop said. "There is always baggage."

"It's coming on a sky-cab," Terry added quickly. The bellhop grunted and stood aside.

"Good thinking," she whispered as they passed it. "I thought we'd have to battle that robot."

"It's called an automaton," Terry corrected her.

"What's the difference?"

"I don't know. That's just what it's called here."

"Got it. Aw-tah-mah-ton," she repeated.

The inside of the hotel was as shabby as the outside. There were water stains and bald spots on the carpet, cracks in the plaster, and practically an inch of dust on the floor.

No footprints in the dust, Gadget noted. *That means we're the first ones here in a long time. If we find treasure and get out before any of the other teams find it, we'll win. Or at least we won't lose.*

Another wooden man stood at the front desk. In front of him was an enormous open book, also covered with dust. The automaton woke as they approached.

"Greetings—greetings—greetings—" he repeated.

Gadget glanced back at Terry. "Have you run into any broken automatons yet?"

"Nope. Maybe give it a whack—that's what my dad does to our TV."

She reached over and hit the automaton on the shoulder. The movement knocked it out of its loop.

"We currently have no vacancies," it said in an automated voice. "Sorry for the inconvenience! Next time make a reservation!"

"How can there be no vacancies?" Terry asked from behind her. "This place is deserted!"

"Sorry for the inconvenience!" the clerk repeated.

"We don't need any rooms," Gadget said. "I just want to ask about a former guest."

"Sorry! We do not give out any personal information! We are most discreet—most discreet—" the machine said again and again.

Gadget reached over and gave it another knock, but this time she accidentally pushed it over. It crashed to the floor with the sound of blown springs.

"Oops," Gadget said when the automaton didn't get up. "Well, let's have a look at the guest registry." She pulled the big book around and brushed the dust off to read the faded ink. She flipped back through the pages until she saw the name *Weston Fawkes*.

She tapped it. "That must be Captain Fawkes's dad. He stayed here sometimes. Thought so. That's why this place is marked on the map."

"So there's no treasure here?" Terry asked.

"Not likely. But there might be a clue. Look." Across from the name was the note *Tower*. "That's where he stayed." She flipped through the pages. "Looks like he was the last one to stay in the tower. Maybe he left something behind?"

"Maybe," Terry said. He frowned. "Does that mean we have to go up in that tower that looks like it's about to collapse?"

"Yep," she said. "Let's go."

Past the desk was a rickety spiral staircase. An automaton knelt in front of it, hammering on the first step. Gadget tried to step over the automaton, but an invisible force stopped her.

"Please use the elevators," the automaton said. "Sorry for the inconvenience." He went back to hammering.

"I'm getting sick of that phrase," she muttered as she tapped the button for the elevator. After a long wait, a door slowly opened. Inside was an automaton elevator operator.

As she and Terry got on, the automaton asked, "Which floor, please?"

"The tower," she answered.

"The twentieth floor," the automaton said. "Up we go!" The elevator groaned to life and slowly made its way up. The elevator came to a halt at the ninth floor, and the door opened.

"Have a nice day!" the elevator operator said.

Gadget peered out from her place in the elevator car. "This is the wrong floor," she said. "We want to go the *tower*."

"This is your floor. Have a nice day!"

"Everything in this place is broken," she grumbled.

"This panel is loose," Terry said. He crouched behind the elevator operator and removed a metal plate. Inside was a tangled mess of wires and bolts.

"I bet we have to rewire it," Gadget said, studying it. The wires emerged on the left side of the panel and connected to one or more of the bolts on the right side.

"I don't know what to make of this," Terry said.

"It's actually not too much of a mess, if you know what you're looking at." She fiddled with the wires and bolts for a few minutes before finally rearranging the wires in what she hoped was the correct order.

"Take us to the tower, please," she tried again.

"Up we go!" The operator said, and the elevator groaned to life, taking them all the way to the top.

Gadget stepped off the elevator onto a

small landing with a single door, which was opened a crack. She pushed it all the way open.

"The penthouse is being cleaned!" an automaton maid told her. It was wiping at a mirror with a gray cloth that was full of holes. "Sorry for the inconvenience."

"I don't mind if you clean while I'm here," Gadget said, stepping into the room. Terry followed her in.

"Please wait while the room is being cleaned," said the robot again. "Sorry for the inconvenience."

Ignoring the robot, they searched the room. It didn't take long. The room wasn't clean, but it was empty. Nothing in the drawers and closet. Nothing under the bed or behind the dresser.

Terry sighed. "Guess we wasted our time coming here."

"Yeah," she admitted.

The maid was still swiping at the filthy mirror.

There's something written on that cloth, Gadget realized.

"Let's head to another location," Terry said eagerly. He took out his map and squinted at it. "It's too dark to read in here. Let's get back outside."

"I want to see one more thing."

"Don't take too long. I'm going to go look at my map in the sunlight." Terry hurried out of the room while Gadget approached the maid.

"I can finish cleaning the mirror," she said. "You can take a break."

"Really?" The automaton handed her the cloth. "A break?"

"Sure."

"I've never had a break!"

"Well, knock yourself out."

The automaton maid hummed happily to itself.

Gadget unfolded the cloth and took a better look. The writing she'd seen was initials: the letters *WF* stitched into the cloth.

It could stand for Weston Fawkes, she thought. *And these holes in the cloth look snipped out, not like random rips.* She laid out the map on the bed and put the cloth on top of it. She rotated the cloth, flipped it over, and rotated it again. The eight holes in the cloth now revealed eight of the marks on the map.

It's a decoder! I bet this shows where the treasures are. That gives me a huge edge on the others. I mean 'us,' she corrected herself. She'd already forgotten about Terry. *But do I want to tell him?* She memorized the eight locations revealed on the map. She decided a snail-shaped island in the harbor would be her first destination. It was closest to the hotel and far enough away from the city center that they probably wouldn't land themselves in a battle with other pirates.

I don't have a treasure yet, but I'm making progress, she thought as she put her map back in her bag.

The automaton was still humming to itself.

"Break time is over," Gadget said. She handed the cloth back to the maid.

"Oh," the maid said sadly.

"Sorry for the inconvenience." Gadget left the room and pushed the elevator call button repeatedly with no luck.

She started down the stairs. *Twenty floors,* she thought grimly, *but down is easier than up. Hope Terry doesn't get sick of waiting and take off without me . . .*

She reached the bottom and jumped over the railing to avoid the automaton carpenter still banging on the bottom step. When she hit the floor she realized there were four strangers dressed in what looked to be some kind of military uniform standing in the lobby, and two of them were holding Terry.

CHAPTER 4

Terry was struggling to get free, kicking helplessly while the soldiers held his arms. "What are you doing here?" the commander asked. He had a red face and a drooping moustache.

"None of your business!" Terry snapped.

"This is a known lair for pirates and other criminals," the commander replied. "As an officer of the Verne Aero-Navy, that means it *is* my business!"

The soldiers were circled around Terry with their backs to the stairs.

I could sneak past them and leave, Gadget thought. *Or I could try to rescue him, which would probably mean getting caught myself. Either way I have to decide fast.*

She crept past them, crawling behind the desk and over the body of the fallen desk clerk.

"Sorry, no vacancies," the clerk still muttered as she passed. "Next time make a reservation." Gadget reached the door and addressed the doorman.

"Can you please get my baggage?" she said. "It's right there." She pointed at the commander. The giant automaton nodded.

"My pleasure, ma'am!" The bellhop stomped over and scooped up the commander. The other soldiers jumped back in surprise. Terry broke free from their grasp and reached for his sword.

"Bring that to the bottom of the mountain," Gadget told the bellhop. The bellhop nodded and carried the commander out of the room.

"Don't just stand there!" the commander shouted. "Help me!" The other soldiers ran after the giant automaton to rescue their leader.

"Smart thinking. Thanks," Terry said. "Did you find any treasure?"

I should tell him what I did find, but we're in a hurry. She shook her head. "No. We better get out of here fast!"

They bolted across the lawn to the cloud-skimmer. A moment later they were soaring across the outskirts of Verne.

LEVEL 2

CHAPTER 5

"Where are we going?" Terry shouted.

"The harbor!" she yelled back. One of the eight spots on the map was right in the middle of the bay, on a little rock far from shore. She was nervous about landing on such a tiny space but didn't have time to worry about it.

Their path to the bay brought them through more mountains. Terry yelped as Gadget took sharp corners and flew into tight passages between cliffs, but at last they sailed past the mountains and over the harbor. A small, rocky beach surrounded the bay. The water was roiling.

"What are you doing?" Terry cried as she flew past the beach and continued over the water.

"You'll see!" The small, snail-shaped island came into view, and she started their descent. She braked and this time made a soft landing on the island. She got off and looked around.

"There's nothing here," Terry said. He was right—the rocky island had no grass or trees, and the surface was too hard for anything to be buried there. "That's two dead ends in a row," he complained.

Gadget narrowed her eyes. *This is why I don't like working in groups. Seems like I do all the work and just get criticized. Guess I'll keep that decoder to myself.*

Terry slid up to the driver's seat. "I want to pick the next destination." As he nudged the cloud-skimmer forward, Gadget noticed a thin crack forming a perfect circle at the very center of the island. She'd missed it before because the cloud-skimmer had been directly on top of it.

"Look!" She pointed. Terry got off the cloud-skimmer and saw it too. They hauled the machine aside. Terry dropped to his knees and ran his fingers along the circle. "How do we open it?"

"I don't know."

Terry leaned back on his knees and pointed at a boulder. "Maybe if we both push, we can move that. See if there's anything under it."

"Good idea." Together, they were able to roll it over, revealing a crank. Terry turned the crank, grunting with effort. The round door slid open.

"Bingo!" Gadget cheered. She hurried over and peered into the hole. Water slapped at the lip of the hole. Terry crouched down and reached into the water, deeper and deeper until his sleeve was wet to the shoulder.

He stood up and shook the water off. "It's too deep. Somebody has to go in."

"Hullo!" shouted a voice behind them. Gadget turned and saw what looked like a spaceman waving at them. He had a fishbowl-style helmet and a baggy, gray body suit. Tubes led from the helmet to the back of the suit.

This game just got weird, she thought.

The spaceman removed his helmet. "How lovely! I see you have one of those sky-hoppers."

"Cloud-skimmer," Terry corrected. "What are you wearing?"

"It's an underwater exploring suit."

"I'll let you take a ride on the cloud-skimmer if I can try that diving suit," Gadget said.

"It's a deal!" The diver started to take off the outfit.

"I could go," Terry offered.

"I'll be fine," she said.

While she climbed into the suit, Terry showed the diver how to use the cloud-skimmer. Gadget put on the helmet and lowered herself into the water.

When she hit the bottom about twenty feet down, she found a tunnel. A light on her helmet flipped on automatically and lit up the path. She walked along the ocean floor, hopping over urchins and avoiding spiny fish and a giant octopus. The octopus grabbed her, and she nearly lost her breathing pack as she frantically wriggled free. She couldn't reach her sword with the diving suit on, so she had to punch the creature in the head. The octopus blinked and swam away.

At last she found a ledge and climbed up out of the water into a cavern. She found herself face-to-face with a skeleton. Its bony hands held an intricate-looking safe covered in gears and dials.

The skeleton turned its head to face her. It stood up and lurched toward her.

She backed up, unzipping the diving suit so she could reach her sword. As the skeleton reached for her, she took a big swing with the sword and knocked its arm out of the way. The skeleton growled and leaped at her. She swung the sword again and again, knocking the skeleton into pieces. At last its fragmented body fell to the ocean floor. Then Gadget noticed a skeleton key hanging around its neck on a chain.

"Sorry, Bones," she said and grabbed the key. "You won't need this anymore."

She unlocked the safe, and it opened, the gears turning and spiraling. Inside she found a metal cylinder with grooves on one end. It looked like part of a machine.

I was expecting gold or jewels, but treasure is treasure. She slid the part into her pouch.

Maybe Captain Fawkes will know what it is. And pay me for my half, since we're not going to cut it in two.

LEVEL 3

CHAPTER 6

I'm up a level, but better yet I have a treasure. If I can just hang on to it, I'll get out of this game. She zipped the diving outfit back up, put on the helmet, and made her way back through the watery tunnel to the island.

As she climbed out of the hole she heard a noise overhead. She looked up. *Did the diver come back with our cloud-skimmer?*

A craft appeared over the bluffs and started for the island. It looked like a rowboat dangling from a small zeppelin. She could see several pirates on board. *That must be a sky-skiff,* she thought.

Terry was pacing back and forth on the far

side of the island, looking out to sea.

I need to warn him! She jumped up and down, waving and shouting.

"Terry!" she shouted. "I mean, TerribleT!"

He must have heard her, but he didn't turn around. The sky-skiff passed over her head and landed on the far side of the island. She ran toward it, ready to fight. A bearded man leaped out and shook hands with Terry.

"Thanks for sending out a signal, partner," the man said.

Gadget stopped in her tracks. *What? Terry sent for them? How? And why?*

"She has treasure," Terry said, pointing her way.

She shook her heard. "I went looking for treasure, but there wasn't any."

"She's lying, Mike," a woman in the skiff shouted. "She's holding out on us!"

"You wouldn't hold out on Menacing Mike, would you?" the pirate asked.

Gadget touched the hilt on her sword. *I can't fight them. It would be four against two. Five against one, if Terry fights on their side.*

"There's no need to fight when you can join our crew," the pirate said. "You'll get a piece of the prize. And since you have a knack for finding things, you'll be a good crewmate."

Well, at least I won't have to worry about losing, she thought. She took the cylinder out of her bag and handed it to Mike. He looked at it and smiled. "Oh, yes. This is what he's looking for all right."

"What is it, Mike?" asked Terry.

"No time to explain," the crew leader said. "Now come on. We have lots of exploring to do, and the captain isn't friendly when he gets impatient."

Gadget followed them to the skiff. The woman helped Mike and Terry climb back in, but as Gadget grabbed the edge, the skiff suddenly rose a few feet in the air. The woman laughed at her.

"Sorry," she said with a sneer. "It looks like we're out of room."

Her former partner wouldn't look at her. He had huddled down in the skiff the second he got on board.

"I'll get you for this, TerribleT!" she yelled. "Now I know the *T* stands for 'traitor!'" He didn't answer. The skiff rose high into the air.

I still have one thing nobody else does, she thought. *I know which spots on the map have treasure.*

But as the skiff soared away she realized something else.

I know where to go but have no way to get there.

She put the diving gear back on and this time went to the shore. She had to fight the currents while avoiding sharp rocks and spiked fish. When she dragged herself onto the rock beach, she was exhausted.

"It's about time you returned my underwater exploration outfit," a man said.

"Huh?" She looked up and saw a very old man in a small shack with a window. A sign read AIRSHIP AND BOAT RENTALS. There were sky-skiffs on a rack and other vehicles she didn't recognize. She saw a second sign that read NEW! UNDERWATER EXPLORING OUTFITS. The sign hung near diving outfits like the one she was wearing hanging from a rack.

"Oh." *That diver traded us something that didn't even belong to him!* "Can I swap this for a boat?" she asked.

"You can't trade what's already mine," the man said. "Now off with it. Off with it."

As Gadget stepped out of the diving gear, she looked around the room. Her eyes landed on a strange contraption off to the side that read OUT OF ORDER. It was spherical and made of metal and thick glass.

"What's that?"

"That's my Narwhal," he said. "It's my favorite piece of equipment, but it's broken."

"What's a Narwhal?"

"An underwater boat."

Aha. A submarine. "If I fix it can I borrow it?"

"Why, certainly."

She went over to get a better look. The ball-shaped hunk of metal and glass was about four feet wide. She peered inside and saw it would be a tight fit for even one person.

She opened a small door on the side and found a number of tiles with circuits crisscrossing and twisting across them. The circuits between tiles didn't match up. But she found one loose tile she pried off, and then she could slide the rest around.

She slid the tiles until the parts started to match up. Some pieces could match up in different ways, so there was a lot of trial and error before she finally got them all arranged correctly. Finally she snapped the loose tile back into place and it fit perfectly.

She slammed the door and threw the switch. The submarine made a gentle hum.

"I got it working!" she told the man.

"Fair enough. You can have it for one hour," he replied.

I'll try to get it back, she thought, *but I have a feeling it won't be in an hour*. She pushed the machine into the water and climbed inside, pulling the lid down above her head. There were four levers inside. She tested each to see how it worked. One rotated the machine right and left, one moved it back and forth, and the third moved it up and down.

And what does this one do? she wondered, pulling the last lever. A long, narrow spike emerged from the front. As she held the lever down, the spike started to spin.

No wonder it's called a Narwhal. It has a horn, just like the sea creature.

She looked at her map, focusing on one of the X marks she knew had a treasure. She could get there by water if she could find her way across the bay and into the canals.

Maybe this time I can get away with the treasure before a rival gang shows up, she thought as she set out. As she traveled, she realized she could use the horn as a drill to break through any rocks or debris that got in her way. That would at least keep her on a relatively straight path. A shark came toward her, but she was also able to use the horn as a weapon to scare the creature away. When she found herself in a narrow channel, she knew she had navigated correctly. She entered the canal that ran through the city. She had to scoot the submarine along the bottom edge of the canal to avoid getting crushed by the hulls of bigger boats.

She made a turn into an even narrower canal and found a tunnel that led into a building. This was where the *X* was marked on her map.

She brought the submarine to the surface and threw open the lid. The tunnel led deeper into the building. From somewhere within, Gadget could hear rumbling, hissing, and the roar of what sounded like fire. Clouds of steam leaked through some heavy doors.

This is where they turn water into steam, she realized. *The city runs on steam power.*

She carefully steered the submarine over to a ladder and climbed out onto a concrete pier. Three massive words had been painted along the walls but were faded and hard to read.

VERNE STEAM WORKS

Looking around, she saw several curved pipes that emerged from the floor and disappeared into the walls. *The steam must travel through those pipes and all over the city. But where's the treasure?*

There were small doors on each of three walls. She tried one and found herself in a smaller room with several valves. They didn't have the hand wheels that valves usually do.

Instead, they had big bolts that probably required a special wrench to move.

Gadget tried the second door and found herself in a maze of tunnels and pipes. The pipes hissed and some blew jets of hot steam sideways across the corridor.

It's impossible to see in there with all the steam, she thought. *I need to turn off the steam, which means I need a wrench, which means the third room must have one.*

The third room did have a wrench. Unfortunately it was in the hand of a worker who turned and glared at her. She was the same age as Gadget but much taller. The girl slapped her palm with the wrench. She wore high-waisted pants, suspenders, and a billowy shirt. Resting on top of her head was a pair of thick goggles.

"Who are you?" the girl asked.

"Um, Gadget," she said.

"I'm Maggie, and I work here. We don't like intruders here at Verne Steam Works."

CHAPTER 7

"I'm lost," Gadget said, trying to sound helpless. "I came in through the water tunnel by mistake and need directions."

Maggie wagged the wrench at her. "How did you miss all the signs that said 'keep out' and 'no trespassing'?"

"I was underwater. In a Narwhal." She shrugged.

"What's a Narwhal?" Maggie was still holding the wrench but now looked curious rather than threatening. If she didn't know the term, Gadget figured she must be a real player, not an NPC.

"It's a submarine. Really small and easy to operate."

"No kidding? Can I see it?"

"Sure!" Gadget was just happy Maggie wasn't shaking the wrench in her face anymore. She waved her hand back the way she'd came. "It's in this room."

"You go first," Maggie said. She held up the wrench again, as a reminder of who was in charge. Gadget led the way back to the first room. They stepped out on the pier. The Narwhal still floated right where Gadget had left it, next to the ladder.

"I've been stuck in this room since I started," Maggie said in a low voice, revealing that she was a real person. "I'm kind of dying to get out and explore."

"Do you want to sneak out in the Narwhal?"

"Really? You'd let me do that?"

"Yeah. Actually you would be doing me a big favor if you took it back to the rental place. It's on the beach of the harbor."

"I shouldn't," said Maggie. "I'll probably get into more trouble than it's worth."

I don't want her to get into trouble, thought Gadget. *But I don't want to lose the game either.*

"Come straight back," Gadget said, "and if anyone asks, tell them you were returning a lost Narwhal you found."

"That could work," Maggie said. "Sorry I didn't trust you at first. I was told to watch out for pirates, and, well, seeing how you're dressed . . ."

"No problem," Gadget said with a shrug. "You're just doing your job."

"So how do I operate this thing?" Maggie asked.

Gadget explained the levers and told her how to reach the bay. A few minutes later Maggie dove down in the submarine and disappeared.

There's one person I wouldn't mind having on my team, Gadget thought. *Too bad she's not a pirate.*

Maggie had left the wrench sitting on the pier. Gadget picked it up and went back to the valve room. She started turning off all the valves, but then she noticed a meter on the wall. Each time she turned off a valve, the needle jerked to the right. It was already well into the red DANGER area.

She quickly opened the valves again. *I have to figure out which valves to turn off.* She checked the pipe room and noted which pipes were spitting steam. Then she returned to the valve room and shut off just those pipes.

She made her way through the maze of corridors to a platform elevator. She threw the switch. The elevator didn't start. She went back to the valve room and turned on the steam halfway for the pipe powering the elevator, then hurried back. She hit the button and the elevator groaned to life.

It took her down a floor to a small cellar. The room was damp and the walls were covered with mold. Gadget spotted another safe in the shadows. As she stepped toward it, several rats came out of a grate and gnashed their teeth.

She drew her sword and swung it at the first rat, knocking it out of her way. Then she turned and swiped at the other two. She killed them both, but more came pouring in, rushing at her with teeth and claws. One carried a key in its mouth. She hacked and slashed until they were all gone and the last rat dropped the key to the safe.

She opened the safe. Inside was a doughnut-shaped metal device. *The cylinder I found earlier must fit into this, but what is it? What does this thing do when we find all the parts and put it together?*

LEVEL 4

CHAPTER 8

Gadget put the device in her pouch and stepped onto the platform elevator. But when she threw the switch again, the elevator strained and wouldn't lift her. It wasn't getting enough power with the steam turned halfway off. She'd have to find another way to get to the next floor.

She found a crate in the corner and pushed it over to the elevator. By climbing on top of the crate, she was able to climb up the elevator shaft and pull herself up to the main floor.

She hurried back toward the main room of the warehouse but slowed as she approached the door. *After I found the decoder for the map, there were Aero-Navy soldiers waiting for me. When I found the first treasure, there were pirates. Who's out there this time? And can I avoid them completely?*

She pressed her ear to the door and heard voices.

"Split up and explore everything!" roared a man. "We're almost out of time. Six of the eight treasures have already been found."

Seven, she thought, but she wasn't going to let them find out about the one in her bag. She turned around and ventured back into the tunnels. Soon she heard voices behind her.

"Hey, that's a deckhand from the *Zephyr*!"

"Get her!"

Gadget broke into a run.

A moment later she reached a junction of pipes and valves on the wall. She took the wrench from her pouch and closed all the valves, then sprinted farther down the tunnel. Behind her she heard a muffled explosion and startled cries. The steam had built up in the pipes and burst them. She hoped that would slow down the men chasing her.

If I can get back to the Zephyr and hand in my treasure, I'll win the game, she thought.

She reached a dead end and wheeled around. Two pirates emerged from the darkness, both frazzled and damp from the steam explosion.

"There you are!" the tall one shouted.

"That was a mean trick!" the short one said.

"You wouldn't do it if you didn't have a treasure," the tall one continued. "If you surrender it now, we'll let you escape."

"No!" Gadget said. "I worked hard for it." *I found it. I solved the puzzle to get it. I fought off the rats. I even struck the deal with Maggie.*

"Tell you what," the tall pirate said. "Join my crew. We could use a resourceful crewmate like you. One who can locate treasure and take out experienced fighters like Pudge and me."

"I don't trust you," she said. "Menacing Mike already robbed me once."

"How about we pirate-shake on it?" asked the tall pirate.

The one he called Pudge nodded. "Good idea, Hal."

Hal offered her his hand. Gadget stepped over and grasped it. He clutched her hand and a moment later had her arm twisted behind her back and his other elbow around her neck.

Gadget groaned. "Oh, come on!" she shouted through clenched teeth. "Isn't anyone here trustworthy?"

Pudge reached into her pouch and grabbed the machine part she'd just found. "What's this supposed to be?"

"I don't know, but it's what we're looking for," Hal said. He pushed her away. "Thanks for your help, deckhand. See you on the *Zephyr*—good luck facing the captain's wrath when you show up empty-handed."

I should turn them both in, she thought as they strolled away, chuckling between themselves. *I would do it if I dared talk to those Aero-Navy soldiers again.*

But she had a more important goal than revenge. *I have to find the last piece of treasure. And it sounds like there's only one left.*

CHAPTER 9

After exploring the tunnels, Gadget found a ladder. She climbed up, pushed a grate aside, and clambered out into what looked like the boiler room of a large building. Steam pipes branched into smaller pipes and disappeared into the ceiling.

There was a tattered blueprint of the Steam Works building taped to the wall. She could see that the building was shaped like the letter *H*, with a fat middle bar. She searched her own map until she found a building of the same shape. She remembered that one of the treasures was less than a mile away. On her map, the building was shown with a clock face.

She thought of the tower she'd seen way back at the beginning of the game with the stopped clock.

But how do I get there from here? For starters, how do I get out of here? She checked the blueprint for the nearest exit and took off in that direction.

At last she saw a set of glass doors and burst through them onto a bustling street. Steam-powered carriages chugged along like tiny trains off the rails. Delivery robots sped along on built-in wheels. People stood along the edges of buildings selling newspapers, fruit, and gadgets.

She was about to plunge into the streets when the people all fled to the sides of the buildings. A steam-puffing vehicle came storming down the street, something between a train and a tank. It screeched to a halt and Aero-Navy soldiers spilled out. The red-faced commander she'd seen at the inn barked orders at two dozen henchmen.

"Search the area! Arrest anyone who looks like a pirate!"

Gadget frowned. *I look like a pirate.* She headed back for the stairs and went up another flight, then another. She could hear soldiers in the building shouting to one another, their footsteps echoing up the stairs from below.

She reached the eleventh floor and found a room with large windows. She peered out at the city and saw the streets were still packed with soldiers. But she also saw rails connecting the buildings. A cart came flying in on one of the rails and jolted to a stop. A bell rang, and moments later several messenger boys and girls filed into the room. They sorted the piles of envelopes and folders, shoved them into tote bags, and hurried out again.

In the distance she could see the clock tower. The clock was still stopped at two minutes to twelve.

Gadget heard soldiers on the stairs getting closer.

She flipped a switch and jumped into a cart as it started rolling. It rolled along the rail, hit a slope, and moments later she was speeding downward in midair.

The cart hit the lowest part of the dip and rumbled slowly back up. Gadget gripped the sides of the cart, hoping it wouldn't tip over.

The cart reached the top of the rail and zoomed down again, this time taking a hard curve. She leaned to the right to keep the cart from flipping off the track. She shifted her weight back and forth as the rail zigged and zagged.

The cart sped up again as it approached a fork. To the left, Gadget could see the majestic tower with the broken clock. To the right was something that looked like a fort.

That must be the military headquarters, or maybe a prison, she thought. *I need to go left, to the clock tower.* As she approached the fork she threw her weight to the left and forced the cart to scoot over to the new rail. She realized too late that this rail was damaged. There was a four-foot gap between rails. She was about to plunge to her death.

Gadget threw her weight up and made the cart hop across the gap. It landed on the rail opposite the gap and scooted into the big, colorful building.

The cart braked hard and tipped, spilling her to the floor. A bell rang. Soon she was surrounded by a dozen children wearing short pants and long socks and buckled caps with short brims. They seemed to range between nine and thirteen years old.

"What are we supposed to do with her?" one asked.

"Turn her in to the Verne Aero-Navy," said an older boy who was dressed differently than the rest. He wore a vest with a tie and a pair of thick, round glasses. Judging by his confident posture, Gadget guessed he was the group's ringleader. "She's a pirate. There's a reward for collaring pirates."

Gadget drew her sword. "That's right. I'm a pirate. Aren't you afraid?" *I sure hope you are because I don't want to fight kids.*

"You're pretty small for a pirate," one of the girls said.

"She's only a few years older than I am," a boy added.

"I'll bet she doesn't even know how to use that sword," yet another boy said.

"I do too!" Gadget protested. She swiped the sword as if that would show she could use it.

"Prove it, then," the ringleader said, crossing his arms. "We'll give you a challenge. If you lose, we'll turn you in for the reward."

"Good idea, Archie!" said the girl.

"What if I win?"

"Then we don't turn you in," Archie said.

"Not good enough," she said. "I need one of you to show me where something is in this building."

Archie paused, thinking it over. "I'll take you anywhere you want to go."

"Great." She realized she didn't know what the challenge *was*. "What do I have to do?"

"We have to open all these envelopes," Archie said. "We'll throw them in the air and you open them with your sword. If you get one hundred before you miss three, you win. If you don't, we're turning you in."

"Sounds like fun." *Wish I'd practiced with my sword more*, she thought.

It started easily, with Archie lobbing a single envelope in the air. Gadget slashed at it with her blade. She didn't actually open the envelope so much as destroy it, but it didn't seem to matter. A younger boy held up a finger to show she'd scored.

Then other children joined in, flinging envelopes in the air two and three at a time, while others lined up to track her score. She had to speed up her swings and hit as many as she could with each slice. She found herself leaping around, spinning, and diving. She missed one envelope that was out of reach and another she just didn't see.

The final flurry came. She swept the sword frantically, making the envelopes explode into confetti. Too late she saw another one drift to the floor, but when she looked up she saw ten kids lined up, each with both hands up and ten fingers spread. She had gotten a hundred before the third envelope reached the floor.

"I told you I was a pirate," she said to Archie. "Now, there's a treasure in this building. I want you to take me to it."

"Ha!" he said. "If I knew where there was treasure I'd have taken it myself."

"Well, where could it be hidden, then?"

Archie shrugged. "We're all over this building every day. We see every room and know every corner."

"Except . . ." a girl interrupted and then clamped her mouth shut.

Archie turned. "Except what?"

"There's one place nobody ever goes," she said. "The clock tower." She turned to Gadget. "The clock hasn't worked for years, and nobody's even tried to fix it. Who knows what's up there?"

CHAPTER 10

"How do you get to the clock tower?" Gadget asked.

"You can't," Archie said. "That's why nobody's tried to fix it."

"Can you get me as close as you can?"

"Sure. Follow me." Archie ran toward the stairs and started leaping up the steps two at a time. Gadget chased after him. A dozen other children followed her, swept up in the adventure.

If it's been broken for so long, why hurry now? Gadget thought as she tried to keep up. She took a wrong turn a couple of times, but the children behind her pushed her in the right direction.

At last Archie led them through a set of doors to a balcony.

There's nowhere to go from here, she thought. *We must almost be there!*

But she was wrong. To her shock, Archie climbed out on a ledge and started to creep alongside the building.

No way, Gadget thought. Still, she stepped out to the same treacherous ledge. With her back pressed to the wall, she took slow side steps. A row of children came along after her, egging her on.

Archie came to a crawl space and entered. Gadget crept in after him. There were still smaller children right on her heels. They crawled for about twenty feet. At last they reached a round chamber directly below the clock tower.

"The clock's up there, but there's no ladder," Archie said, pointing. Gadget looked up past the gears of the clock and saw a white circle glowing in the shadows. It was the sun shining through the clock face. Four ropes hung down, one dangling all the way to the floor.

This is like Grandma's cuckoo clock, she realized, thinking of the time she took it apart to figure out how it worked. *Weights power the clock by pulling on the ropes, but this one is missing its weights—that's why it's broken. What can we use for weights?*

She noticed that the room was packed with children—at least a dozen of them. She realized what she had to do.

"You," she said to a boy who seemed to be the smallest of the kids. "Climb up the long rope, then jump over to the rope on the far end."

The boy hesitated.

"You're not a coward, are you?" Archie asked.

" 'Course not!" That was all it took to get the boy shimmying up the rope. Gadget sent one kid up after another. She knew from the cuckoo clock that the weights had to be equal. So she sorted the kids into groups, with the same number of tall, small, and medium-sized kids on each rope. Archie nodded at them, encouraging them to do as she said. She had to

make a couple of them swap places, but when
they were divided up perfectly there was a *click*.
The gears had reset.

Now I'll be the pendulum. She grasped the
longest rope, shimmied up a few feet, and
kicked off a beam to start swinging. Dust
rained from the gears above as they grinded to
life. Some of the children yelped, but they all
held on to their ropes. Gadget kept swinging.
A group of bats shot down, their leathery
wings flapping in her face.

"Hold on!" she yelled to the others and
kept swinging. She heard the clockworks
rumbling above, and the clock started to tick.

*The clock has been stuck at two minutes to
twelve,* she thought. *What happens when it
reaches twelve?*

Gadget swung and swung, counting one
hundred and twenty swings. Then there was
another click as something shifted deep in
the mechanism.

A bell started to ring with a deafening
clang. Once, twice, three times. She tried to
peer up into the clockworks as she swung.

High above the gears she saw a door slide open; inside was a cubbyhole with a safe.

She slowed her swings. The bell rang six more times before she was able to stop completely. Now the clock was frozen at exactly twelve. She continued up the rope, climbed hand over hand across a beam, swung over, and entered the cubbyhole.

This safe was unlocked. She opened it and found . . .

Nothing.

Her jaw dropped in shock. *No. It can't be gone. If somebody beat me to it, the clock would have already changed.*

There wasn't much light. Only the dim glow of the sun through the painted glass of the clock face. She ran her hands along the sides and bottom of the safe. At last her fingertips found the edges of a long strip of thick paper lying flat on the bottom. She carefully picked it up and discovered it was full of punch holes.

Computers used to use punch cards to tell them what to do. This must be the program for whatever that machine is. She started to put the paper in her bag and changed her mind, worried it might get crumpled or torn in there. Instead she wrapped the card around her arm, halfway between her wrist and elbow, and pulled her sleeve down over it.

LEVEL 5

CHAPTER 11

Leveling up is fine, Gadget thought. *But what I really want is to have a treasure not get stolen five seconds later.*

The room suddenly darkened. She looked up and saw a large shadow in front of the clock face. The shadow shifted, and she could see the shape of an airship. *Somebody heard the bells and came to investigate. But is that the* Zephyr *or an Aero-Navy ship?*

There was a *boom* of cannons and the clock face shattered, raining shards of white glass down on the city of Verne. Through the jagged hole, Gadget could see the airship better. Now she saw it was definitely an Aero-Navy ship, with the name BOREAS painted on the side of the ship's wooden frame. Crew members were re-loading the cannon.

"Let's get out of here!" she hissed to the kids below, hoping the soldiers wouldn't be able to hear her. It was possible their attackers didn't know for sure that anyone was inside the tower.

She slid down the rope, feeling it burn her hands, and landed with a *thunk* on the floor. Archie was ushering the children into the crawl space. Overhead another cannonball ripped through the clockworks. Chunks of wood and metal fell from the rafters.

All of the kids were gone except Archie. He waved her on. She shook her head and nudged him toward the hole. He nodded and disappeared into the crawl space. Gadget dropped down to follow, but just before she entered, a net dropped down and covered her body. As she struggled to shake it off, the corners were drawn together, forming a sack with her inside.

The net lifted, pulling her back up into the tower. She got her sword free but too late—if she cut through the ropes now, the fall would be too dangerous.

The net was hoisted up onto a sky-skiff. The skiff turned and flew back to the *Boreas*, where soldiers hauled her on board.

"We've caught a pirate, sir," one of the soldiers said.

Gadget looked up to see the red-faced commander glaring down at her. Then a crooked smile crept up his face. "I've seen *this* pirate before."

CHAPTER 12

The soldiers freed her from the net, ripped the bag and sword away from her, and tied her hands. Two guards with drawn swords stood on either side of her.

The commander got into Gadget's face. "First I see you at the Benbow Inn—a known pirate hideout—and now I find you here. There are pirates all over the city, looting and making trouble. What are you up to?"

"She's got this map," a third soldier said, who had been ransacking Gadget's bag. She handed the commander the map.

"This was stolen by Captain Weston Fawkes Junior," he said. He clenched his teeth.

"I should have known you were with that pip-squeak pirate."

Gadget didn't say anything. She couldn't if she wanted to. This was a cut scene, playing out like a short movie, and all she could do was watch.

"Now I'd like to make you pay for what you did at the inn," the commander said, "but you might prove useful to me. Junior wants to follow in his father's footsteps, so we'll let him." A corner of his mouth turned up in a creepy smile. "I know Fawkes is gathering the pieces of a machine that his father hid around the city. But I don't know what the machine does. If you go back to the *Zephyr*, you can find out."

Gadget finally found herself able to talk. "No way," she said.

"You're loyal to the pip-squeak," the commander said with a disapproving frown. "He can't be trusted, you know. Not even by his own crewmates."

"I'm not exactly loyal to him, but I don't see any reason to help you!"

"Because you don't want to spend the rest of your life in a workhouse!" the commander barked. He reached into his pocket. Gadget cringed, expecting him to come out with a weapon, but instead he showed her a small metal bird, like the cuckoo from a steampunk clock.

"Take this messenger." He tried to hand it to her, but her hands were tied, so he handed it to the female soldier, and she slid it into Gadget's pocket.

"It's there whenever you need it," the woman said, in a nicer tone than the commander. "Just give it a message and let it fly. It will find its way home."

Terry must have had one of those, she realized. *That's how he sent word to Mike's crew about where we were. That traitor.*

"I won't do it," she said. *I don't like Fawkes, but I'm not a traitor like Terry.*

"Maybe you need time in the brig to think about it," the commander said.

The soldiers dragged her to the airship's prison, untied her hands, and shut her in a small cell with an iron door and sturdy wooden walls. The only furniture was a hammock, and that was already filled with a hulking body facing the wall. Gadget sat in the corner.

Either I turn into a traitor, or I end up in prison, she thought, resting her chin on her knees. *I don't know what to do.*

The person on the hammock rolled over and spoke in a gravelly voice. "Hey, there. I know you."

Gadget perked up. It was Maggie, the girl from the Verne Steam Works.

"What are you doing here?" Gadget asked.

"I've been accused of stealing a Narwhal." Maggie sat up and put her feet on the floor.

"But you were just returning it . . ."

"I tried to explain that, but they didn't believe me," Maggie said, then she perked up. "But now you can tell them. You'll do that for me, right?"

"Of course," she said. *But I don't think they'll listen.*

"What about you?" Maggie asked. "What are you in for?"

"For being a pirate."

"You're a pirate?" Maggie gasped. "You lied to me!"

"I never said I *wasn't* a pirate," Gadget said. "I said I was lost, and I was."

"Fair enough," Maggie said. "But I shouldn't have left you alone in the Steam Works. Maybe I do deserve to be in here." She sighed heavily.

The door to the brig squeaked open and someone crept in. Gadget sat up. *Terry? What's he doing here?*

Terry held a finger to his lips and pulled a key from his pocket. Without a word, he opened the cell's door. "Come on," he whispered.

Gadget frowned. "What's going on?"

"I'm rescuing you. What do you think?"

"Why?"

"Because I owe you one. Come on, let's hurry."

"I don't trust you," she hissed.

"I don't blame you," he said. "But we don't have time to argue about it."

Well, I do need to get out of here, she thought. *Once we're out, I can get as far away from him as I can.*

"Come *on*," he pleaded.

"I'll come." She looked back at Maggie and stood up, "But we need to rescue *her* too!"

"If I make a run for it, I'll be in ten times as much trouble," Maggie said. "And they'll never believe I was innocent in the first place."

"But I have to leave," Gadget said. "This is my only chance."

"So you're not going to vouch for me," Maggie said sadly.

Gadget bit her lip. "I'll . . . come back."

"Sure you will."

"I will. I promise." *I'll try, anyway.*

"Good luck, then," Maggie said.

"See you soon," Gadget said before she shut the door behind her.

She followed Terry out of the brig and into the airship's cargo hold. They made their way around barrels and crates to the rear end of the airship, where they entered an empty room with cots and gray blankets.

"This is the sick room," he explained. "Nobody's using it right now." He pushed open a window and started to climb out. "Follow me."

Gadget went to the window and saw that a sky-skiff was there, hovering so close behind the Aero-Navy ship it was hidden from the soldiers on board. Terry leaped to the deck and waved her on, but she paused.

The two other pirates on the skiff helped Terry climb aboard. He turned back and waved at her again to follow.

I still don't trust him, Gadget thought. *What if the ship takes off after I make the jump? But then why would he go through this much trouble when I was already out of his way?*

There were footsteps in the hall, right outside the door. No more time to think about it. She climbed up on the sill and jumped. The wind carried her over, so high she nearly flew right over the others' heads, but Terry grabbed her foot and pulled her safely to the skiff.

He did want to rescue me, she thought. *Maybe he really did feel bad for leaving me stranded on that island.*

She looked at the other pirates on the skiff. She recognized them from the standoff at the harbor, but their leader wasn't among them.

"What happened to Mike?" she asked.

"There was a small mutiny after he let our treasure get plundered," Terry explained.

Feeling better knowing that guy wasn't around, Gadget took a seat. *Does that mean Terry is in charge now? Did he arrange the mutiny? Maybe he's better at this game than I thought.*

As the skiff sailed back to the *Zephyr*, she thought about betrayal.

I let Maggie down, she thought. *No, she made her own decision. And for all I know, it was the right decision. Maybe she's safer with the Aero-Navy than a bunch of pirates.*

Gadget looked over her shoulder at the *Boreas* behind them. *But I still feel guilty.*

They landed on the *Zephyr* a moment later.

"We're not even that far from the *Boreas*," she said.

"That's because we're in battle," Terry explained.

Most of the crew had returned and were scurrying around the deck. Captain Fawkes was standing on a barrel, barking orders and looking more menacing than before. To her surprise they were heading for the clock tower with the shattered clock. The *Boreas* was still circling it, cannons out.

"Brace yourselves!" said a woman. "The two of you, grab a dart cannon. One of you can feed. The other can fire!"

Gadget gulped and let Terry pull her over to a cannon. It had a longer, narrower barrel than the cannons she'd seen on ships in movies.

"Which do you want to do?" he asked. "Feed or fire?"

"Um . . ." She didn't know how to do either. "I guess I'll feed." She looked around and saw a large metal crate with feathers sticking out. Those were the darts, stored with the points down. She pulled one out—it was the size of a loaf of bread and much heavier. Gadget lugged it to the cannon and slid it in. Terry was winding a crank, grunting with the effort. When he couldn't turn it anymore he stood back.

"Out of the way!" he shouted. She moved a split second before the dart exploded out of the cannon. It soared over to the *Boreas*, glancing off the side of the ship itself.

"I missed!" Terry said. "Let's try again."

But he hit the ship . . . Gadget thought. She saw Terry reposition the cannon to shoot at a higher angle. *Aha, he's shooting for the big gasbag!*

"We need another dart!" he said impatiently. "You should get ready with the next shot as I'm firing."

"Sorry." She stepped back over to the bin of darts.

I wonder what happens when he hits the gasbag—will it explode? Just deflate and drop? And what will happen to Maggie?

There was a crash behind her. Splinters of wood went flying as one of the darts from the *Boreas* landed behind her. *Guess I don't have time to worry about it*, she thought, jumping into action. *Like it or not, I'm in a battle.*

She grabbed another dart, fed the cannon, and stood aside while Terry wound up the spring. This time the dart struck the side of the *Boreas*'s massive gasbag, but the point didn't quite poke through its thick skin. The third dart from their cannon tore into the fabric, but the gasbag didn't even deflate. Apparently it wasn't that easy to bring down a massive airship.

Darts soared from the *Boreas*, and the *Zephyr*'s own gasbag took a hit. Captain Fawkes ordered a retreat and the damaged airship sailed away. It wobbled like a leaky balloon through the clouds toward the mountains. The *Boreas*, for now at least, did not give chase.

"What was that about?" Gadget asked.

"The last treasure is in that clock tower," said another pirate. "We have to find it. But the soldiers on the *Boreas* had the same idea."

Gadget touched her forearm. Sure enough, the punch card was still there. *We've been battling for a treasure I had up my sleeve the whole time.*

"I—" she almost blurted out that she had it, but she stopped herself. *I'd better give this straight to Fawkes so I get credit.*

Fawkes was holding himself steady at the mast while the *Zephyr* tilted and swayed.

"Captain!" She unraveled the card from her arm and pulled it from her sleeve, then waved it in front of his face. "Is this the treasure we're fighting for?"

"What? How?" He snatched it from her and looked it over with wide eyes, so carefully she wondered if he could read the punch holes.

"This . . ." he said in astonishment. "This is it!" Then, to her surprise, he turned to the pirates standing beside him. "Crewmates! Arrest this girl. She's a traitor to the *Zephyr* and a spy!"

CHAPTER 13

"What?" Gadget stared in disbelief at the pirate captain as the other pirates crowded around her. "No I'm not! I found that fair and square and brought it to you, just like you asked!"

"I heard there's a spy among us, and I know you came here from that Aero-Navy ship," Fawkes said.

"I was being held prisoner!" she protested.

He patted her down and found the clockwork bird in her pocket. "Aha! A messenger bird with the *Boreas* symbol!" he exclaimed. "Proof!"

"They forced me to take it!" she said.

"Like you couldn't have cast it away."

"I forgot about it," she said honestly.

"You're one of them." He stuffed the card in his pocket. "Crewmates," he said. "Make this spy walk the plank!"

Terror grabbed her in its icy grip. *This can't be happening. I played well. I got three treasures and two were stolen from me. It's not fair!*

"I'm not a spy!" she insisted. "Tell him, Terry—TerribleT!"

Her former partner gave her a hard look. "I don't know that she *isn't* a spy," he said. "She didn't tell me anything about a treasure even though I rescued her. And she does have the messenger bird. I think maybe she's a cheat and a spy after all."

"You jerk!" she hollered, but her voice was barely heard over the roaring of two dozen furious pirates. They pushed and shoved her to the side of the ship, where a long wooden board had been rolled out and now extended high over the city.

Regular pirates can at least take their chances against sharks and drowning, she thought. *I'll just fall . . . and I guess it's "game over" for me.*

They shoved Gadget out on the board. The winds whirled around her. The board bent under her weight and she fought just to keep her balance. There was no hope of running back to the ship—the pirates crowded the deck, waving their swords and egging her on.

This can't be it. The game can't be over.

"Any last words?" the pirate captain asked.

"I do have a question," she said coolly. "What does the machine do? If I have to die, I want to know what it was all about."

The captain looked at her, considering. "I know what it's *supposed* to do, but I don't know if it's true," he admitted. "I've been trying to assemble it and I can't."

She perked up. *That's it! That's my way out of this!*

"Let me try!" she pleaded. "I'm good with gadgets."

"If it works, this is the most powerful machine the world has ever known," said the captain. "My father said I could use it to rule mankind. You think I'd trust a spy with it?"

"Might as well let her try," a voice shouted from the crowd. A boy pushed to the front. It was Archie! But now he was dressed as a pirate. *How did he get here?* Gadget pretended she didn't recognize him.

"My new cabin boy has a big mouth," the captain grumbled.

"She is good with machinery," another voice offered. It was Terry, who'd gone from being her partner to her traitor to her rescuer to her partner and back to her traitor all over again. Now apparently he was trying to help her again. *Unless he's up to something else*, she thought.

"I'd let her try to fix the thing, but keep an eye on her," said Terry.

"Hm," the captain said. "I need you on the cannon. Cabin boy, show this spy to the room where we're keeping the treasure and keep watch while she assembles it."

"Will do, Captain!"

Gadget walked back toward the ship, still struggling to keep her balance on the board with the winds hitting her. The pirates grumbled but let her step back to the ship. Archie tugged on her sleeve and dragged her to a room at the front of the ship.

"Sorry about that," he whispered after he shut the door. "I have to keep up appearances."

"Thanks for vouching for me," Gadget whispered back.

"Of course," he said. "You're the one who inspired me to be a pirate!"

"Really?"

"The way you handled your sword, then solved that clock puzzle? It was amazing."

"Well, thanks. But you probably had a better career path before. You could have worked your way up from the mailroom."

"Too dull for me," he said. "Well, you better get to work on that before the captain gets suspicious." He pointed out the pile of mysterious parts. "From what I've heard, Fawkes is pretty ruthless. Especially when he's angry."

She sat down and inspected each piece. She found the cylinder she'd seen earlier and the doughnut-shaped ring. The first screwed into the second, as she suspected. She found a three-legged hinged piece that was clearly meant to connect the ring, but she couldn't figure out which piece to attach first. She had a question about every hinge or switch that could be configured in different ways.

At last she figured out how the first three pieces fit together. But she realized a fourth piece was supposed to thread through the cylinder before she screwed it into the doughnut. She sighed and took everything apart again. This puzzle was maddening. She put it back together with that piece in place and finally saw how a fifth piece fit. The rest quickly fell into place. The machine was complete: a rod set into a round base, with a fan at the other end and a cord running through it that attached to a spindle.

"You can go get the captain," she told Archie. "I'm done."

"Aren't you going to turn it on and see if it works?"

"It needs power," Gadget said.

Archie studied the machine a moment.

"Aren't you going to get the captain?" Gadget asked.

"Listen," he said. "I like you so I'll level with you: I'm a spy for the Verne Aero-Navy. My ship is the *Boreas*."

"So you're not a cabin boy?"

"I am today." He looked at her. "You really did inspire me to take up piracy, but I'm doing it as an undercover assignment."

"You're working for that awful commander?"

"He's not that bad when you get to know him," Archie said with a shrug. "If you tell me what this contraption does, I'll make sure he goes easy on you after the Aero-Navy takes over the *Zephyr*."

"I don't know what it does," Gadget admitted. "I figured out how the pieces fit together, but I still don't know what it's for."

"I've got to get a message out before I tell the captain," Archie said. "But you know . . . this reminds me of something else I saw." He snapped his fingers. "The navigation room."

"What about it?"

"There's a slot in the floor, right by the wheel. I asked what it was and nobody could tell me. But this thing would fit perfectly, if you turned it over and gave it a twist. What if we plug it in and see what happens?"

Gadget studied the machine in her hands, slowly turning it over. It wasn't that big or heavy and didn't look like a weapon. *But I should know what it does before I give it to the pirate captain*, she thought. *What if he really does want to rule the world? Maybe it is better off with the Aero-Navy.*

"Come on," Archie urged, heading toward the door. "The navigation room is in the rear of the ship."

Gadget shifted from foot to foot, uncertain. "How are we going to get to the navigation room from here? We'd have to carry this thing past twenty-five pirates!"

Terry burst into the room before Archie could answer. "Are you finished yet?" he demanded. "The captain is getting impatient!"

"Not quite," she said, shifting so the assembled machine was out of Terry's view. "I need more time."

"You have *two minutes*," Terry said. He slammed the door behind him.

The two minutes reminded her of the clock tower, where she'd swung on a rope that needed a pendulum. It gave her an idea. She glanced up and saw a trapdoor in the ceiling.

That must lead to the upper deck, she realized.

She turned back to Archie. "Maybe we could swing across."

CHAPTER 14

Gadget boosted Archie up. He grabbed the handle and pulled the trapdoor open. A ladder dropped. Moments later they were on the upper deck, just below the massive drooping gasbag of the airship. As she'd hoped, there were loose ropes dangling from the gasbag, torn by the darts from the *Boreas*.

Archie went first, leaping out to grab a rope and swinging across. He sent it back to Gadget. She first tied the machine to the rope and sent it over, then swung across herself, over the heads of the pirates.

She looked back and saw Terry and Captain Fawkes enter the room where she'd just been.

"We're going to need a quick escape," she said to Archie. "Go get a sky-skiff and fly it behind the ship. Wait for me there."

"You got it, Captain!" he said and flew out the door.

Gadget rolled her eyes but couldn't help her lips from quirking up into a small smile.

She went to the navigation room, a U-shaped area at the rear of the ship. The steering wheel was here, along with compasses and charts and various dials and gauges. She saw the slot on the floor right away. Archie had been right—it looked like a perfect fit for the machine.

I'd hoped we'd at least get a hint of what this contraption is for, but no such luck, she thought. *Guess we're about to find out.*

She inserted the machine into the slot and heard a hiss of steam as it powered up. The cylinder started to turn, slowly at first, then gradually picking up speed.

The cylinder spun faster and faster, now giving off a high-pitched whine. *And there's no off button*, Gadget realized. *The only way to turn it off is to remove it, and now I'm scared to touch it . . .*

The door burst open and Fawkes rushed in with a handful of pirates waving swords. Gadget raised her fists, expecting a fight, but Fawkes's mouth dropped open when he saw the machine was running.

"You fool!" he exclaimed. "You can't run the chrono-variator without a program!"

"What does it do?" she asked over the noise.

"It turns the *Zephyr* into a time machine!" he shouted back. "But without a program it won't know where to go. It'll blast us back to the beginning of time or to the end of time! Maybe even beyond time itself! I don't know."

He took the punch card from his pocket and handed it to her. "Here's the program my father left us. Put it in."

"Where in time will this send us?"

"I don't know! A time when I'll be able to rule the world, I assume!"

Gadget started to insert the card in the machine and paused. "I almost forgot!" she said. "I found this treasure and you owe me half!" She ripped the card down the middle lengthwise. She handed half back to Fawkes.

She reached her hand out the window and let the other half fly away in the breeze.

Fawkes fell to his knees, his mouth opened in a silent scream. The pirates came at her, but she bolted through the door and sped across the rear deck. With no time to see if Archie had actually come through for her, she leaped over the rail. To her relief, she landed in the sky-skiff waiting for her.

"Where to now, Captain?" Archie asked.

"Back to the *Boreas*!" she said. "Do you know the way?"

"We can follow this," he said. He removed a messenger bird exactly like the one she'd had earlier.

There was a crackling in the air. They looked back and saw the *Zephyr* vanish. The air seemed to collapse around it, sending waves that rocked the skiff in the sky. A moment later the sky was calm.

"Go tell the commander the *Zephyr* is gone," Archie said to the clockwork bird. He released it and it flapped off into the clouds. Gadget steered the skiff and followed the bird.

CHAPTER 15

An hour later the sky-skiff circled the tower where Gadget had started the game. She and Archie and Maggie stepped onto the deck with the glowing L33T C0RP logo. She had been prepared for a fight, but the commander had released Maggie willingly when he found out they'd gotten rid of the *Zephyr*.

The Game Runner materialized and greeted them all. "Welcome back, Gadget, Archrival05, and Maggie727. Three of our first four beta testers are winners," he said. "Not bad."

"Archrival?" Gadget asked, turning to him. "I thought your name was Archie?"

"It is," he said with a teasing grin. "Short for 'Archrival05'!"

"I don't feel like a winner," Maggie said over them. "I barely feel like a survivor."

"Sometimes surviving is as good as winning," the Game Runner said.

"What happened to the people on the *Zephyr*?" Gadget asked. *Especially Terry. He must be the fourth beta tester.*

"Their fate is not as bad as Captain Fawkes feared. They will arrive in a thick forest, with no signs of civilization. They will have to find shelter, hunt for food, and make the best of things. But they'll be fine."

"Is that the future or the past?" Archie asked.

"They'll never know for sure," the Game Runner said. "But as the leader of the only group of people on Earth, Fawkes will get what his father promised. He will rule all mankind."

Unless Terry is already planning a mutiny, Gadget thought.

"I want to play again!" Archie said. "The adventure was just getting exciting when it ended."

"Me too," Maggie added. "I spent most of the game in jail. I'm sure I can do better."

"You can all play again anytime you like," the Game Runner said. "But don't be surprised if it's different—treasures will appear in different places. People who were loyal to you will betray you and vice-versa."

"I'll come back too," Gadget said. "I'll look for the two of you." *In fact, you're the main reason I am coming back*, she thought. "And I'll always be loyal to you two, at least."

"Me too!" Archie agreed.

"And me!" said Maggie. "Maybe the three of us can start together next time."

"That's lovely," said the Game Runner. He waved his hand and all four of them disappeared, whisked back to their separate lives.